DINOBALL

*To my wonderful wife Laura for agreeing to marry me,
even though I proposed in a book about
football-playing dinosaurs – CM*

First published in Great Britain in 2009 by
Piccadilly Press,
A Templar/Bonnier publishing company
Deepdene Lodge, Deepdene Avenue,
Dorking, Surrey, RH5 4AT
www.piccadillypress.co.uk

Text © Ciaran Murtagh, 2010
Illustrations © Richard Morgan, 2010
Cover illustration © Garry Davies
Author photograph © Steve Ullathorne

ISBN: 978 1 84812 099 0

3 5 7 9 10 8 6 4

Printed in the UK by CPI Group (UK) Ltd, Croydon, CR0 4YY

DINOBALL

Ciaran Murtagh

Illustrated by Richard Morgan

Piccadilly

CHAPTER 1

The messenger sprinted down Sabreton High Street as if his life depended on it. Customers eating their breakfast at The Hungry Bone Café watched as he zoomed past their tables towards Charlie Flint's dinopants shop at the end of the street.

'Message for Charlie Flint!' he spluttered, out-of-breath, as he burst into the shop and saluted with a flourish.

Charlie Flint dropped his slicing stone in surprise. 'That's me,' he said, stepping out from behind his workbench.

Charlie had been working on a pair of bright green

dinopants for a brontosaurus all morning. Dinopants were Charlie's most popular invention. They had become the must-have fashion accessory and Charlie's dinopants shop supplied eager dinosaurs with as many pairs as they needed.

The messenger cleared his throat and began. 'I'm Andy Leggit – chief messenger to the town of Sabreton.'

Charlie knew who the messenger was. He was the fastest runner in the whole town, and people only used him if the message was very important indeed.

'I've come here to tell you that Billy Blackfoot can't help in the shop today.' Andy bowed, saluted and scurried off to deliver another urgent message.

Charlie's mind began to race. Charlie's best friends Billy 'The Boulder' Blackfoot and James Tusk always helped out in the dinopants shop. It was nearly the end of the school holidays and Billy had come in every day they were off school. If Billy couldn't come in, he must be in trouble. Charlie had to find out what was going on.

'Come on, Steggy!' called Charlie. 'We have to go and see Billy right away!'

Steggy, Charlie's pet dinosaur, growled happily and scampered out of the shop.

Minutes later, Charlie and Steggy were knocking on the door of Billy's cave. There was some banging and crashing from inside, but eventually Billy opened the door. He looked terrible.

'What's wrong?' asked Charlie.

But before Billy had the chance to reply, a baby allosaurus leapt from the cave opening and knocked Charlie to the ground. The excited allosaurus bent over and covered Charlie in sloppy licks.

'Sorry, Charlie!' said Billy, helping his friend to his feet. 'I could only afford a short message to you, so I couldn't explain things fully. This is Fang. He's my new pet dinosaur and he's been here since last night. He's so naughty Mum made me stay at home to make sure he didn't get up to any mischief. Goodness knows what she'll do when I have to go back to school. He's a bit of a handful.'

'So I see,' said Charlie, dusting himself down.

Billy turned and wagged his finger at the baby allosaurus. 'Naughty Fang!'

The dinosaur tucked his tail between his legs and scurried off to say hello to Steggy.

'I can't believe your mum's finally let you have a dinosaur!' said Charlie.

Billy had wanted a pet dinosaur for ages but his mum had always said no.

'He might not be staying!' barked a voice from inside the cave. It was Billy's mum. 'If he doesn't learn how to behave by the end of the summer holidays he'll be out on his very scaly ear. If you ask me, pets are nothing but trouble!'

Steggy narrowed his eyes and swished his tail angrily. Sometimes humans needed reminding that not all pets were trouble – he'd even rescued Charlie on a few occasions.

'Not this one,' said Billy, rushing over to give his mum a big cuddle. 'He'll be no trouble at all.'

'That's what you said about the pet lizard I got you last summer solstice, but who ended up cleaning his cage every morning?'

'But lizards are so boring,' protested Billy. 'It'll be different with a dinosaur. I promise.'

'And where have I heard *that* before, Billy Blackfoot?! Before you know it, he'll be chewing our fine leaf-stuffed sofas and weeing on my best rug! And he's so lively – he kept us up half the night wanting to play.'

'But he's an orphan,' pleaded Billy. 'You've got to be kind to him.'

'How do you know he's an orphan?' asked Charlie.

'I found him yesterday while I was out practising my tracking skills,' explained Billy. 'He was stuck in the Bog of Ooze.'

'The Bog of Ooze!' gasped Billy's mum. 'You didn't tell me that! What have I told you about playing there?'

Nobody in Sabreton went near the Bog of Ooze if they could help it. It was a very dangerous place. The ground looked safe enough, but if you stepped on it, you got stuck fast.

'I wasn't *playing*, I was *tracking* and if I hadn't pulled them out, then the two of them would still be stuck there. It's a good job I'm so muscly!' said Billy, flexing his arms proudly.

'Hold on a minute,' said Charlie. 'Did you say *two*?'

Before Billy had a chance to explain, there was a rumble and a cloud of dust appeared to be making its way up the hill towards them. Over the noise, Charlie could hear James shouting, 'Out of the way! Run! He's gone mad!'

Through the dust, Charlie could see another baby allosaurus. James had both arms wrapped around its neck and was clinging on for dear life.

'They're twins,' explained Billy. 'James has always wanted a pet dinosaur too, so I thought we could look after one each. I suppose we should have checked with our parents first. His one is called Fing.'

'He's going to drag me all the way to Tuskville at this rate!' yelled James.

Fing seemed even more of a handful than his brother and when Fing spotted Fang, he screeched to a halt. James lost his grip and flew through the air. 'Argh!' he screamed as he landed with a splash in a muddy puddle.

Charlie and Billy roared with laughter.

'That dinosaur is *so* naughty!' moaned James. 'He won't do anything I tell him!'

Billy's mum stuck her head out of the kitchen

window. 'You see?' she tutted. 'Nothing but trouble!
Now get them out of my garden before they trample
my flowers!'

Charlie, Billy and James looked at each other.

'Fancy a game of football?' suggested Billy, scooping
his ball off the ground. 'Fing and Fang can wait by the
side of the pitch.'

Charlie and James looked at each other and smiled.
They could never resist a game of football.

CHAPTER 2

The boys walked through the centre of town to get to the football pitch. It soon became clear to Charlie how much of a handful Fing and Fang really were. Fing snatched a mammoth steak off the plate of a customer sitting outside The Hungry Bone Café when no one else was looking, while Fang was so friendly that he ran up to everyone and covered them in sloppy licks – including the boys' teacher, Mrs Heavystep! Mrs Heavystep hit the naughty dinosaur on the head with her handbag and glared at the boys. They hoped it wouldn't mean extra homework when they went back to school the following week.

They were all relieved when they finally got to the football pitch.

'I'm glad you two have got Fing and Fang,' said Charlie as he looked at the dinosaurs sitting in the shade of a tall tree to watch. 'Steggy will have someone to keep him company while we play football.'

'I just hope Fang learns to behave,' said Billy, 'If he keeps on like this my mum won't let me keep him.'

'He *is* pretty naughty,' said James, shaking his head in disapproval.

'You can talk!' spluttered Billy. 'Fang may cover everyone in slobber but at least he doesn't steal their food!'

Charlie smiled. Up till then he had been the only one of his friends lucky enough to have a pet dinosaur. Steggy had been quite mischievous when he was little, but Charlie was sure that the baby dinosaurs would soon grow out of their bad behaviour, like Steggy had.

'Three and in?' suggested Billy, kicking the ball towards the centre circle.

Soon the game was in full swing. By lunchtime, Charlie had scored two goals and Billy was using every trick he could think of to stop his friend scoring the winner. Meanwhile, James was bobbing up and down the goal line and darting from left to right trying to anticipate where the next shot was coming from.

The children were so caught up in the game they didn't notice Fing getting more and more excited on the sideline. When James kicked the ball in Fing's direction, the young dinosaur couldn't contain himself any longer – he yelped with excitement and scurried on to the pitch.

'No!' shouted James when he saw what was happening. But it was too late – Fing had the ball at his feet.

Fang saw what was going on and chased after his brother, swiping the ball with his tail.

'Stop that!' commanded Billy sternly, but Fang was too excited to listen.

'Do something!' called James.

'Your dinosaur started it!' snorted Billy. '*You* do something!'

'*I'll* do something,' huffed Charlie, as he marched towards the naughty dinosaurs.

When Fing saw Charlie he thought it was all part of the game and he knocked the ball further away. Charlie ran after it but he couldn't catch up with the two dinosaurs. Fang dived for the ball and gripped it with his teeth.

'No!' shouted Charlie. 'It's a *foot*ball, not a mouthball!'

It was Steggy who finally came to the rescue. He stormed on to the pitch and growled at the baby dinosaurs angrily. When Fang saw how cross Steggy was he stopped what he was doing and smiled sheepishly, the ball still between his teeth.

POP!

The ball burst in Fang's mouth and flopped to the ground, flat as a slobbery pancake.

'That's just brilliant,' huffed Billy, examining his ruined ball.

Fang growled softly and gave Billy a big lick as if to say sorry.

Billy patted him. 'How can I stay angry at you?' he said, smiling.

'I guess that's the end of that then,' said James, as they all walked off the pitch.

'They're only naughty because they're babies, you know,' said Charlie as they headed for home. 'They'll soon grow out of it.'

'I hope you're right,' said Billy. 'It's school next week, and Mum won't be pleased if he's too naughty to be left alone.' He looked at Fang who was play-fighting with Fing. He shook his head sadly. 'But at this rate, I'll be lucky if she lets him stay at all.'

CHAPTER 3

By Saturday, the baby dinosaurs were just as badly behaved as ever. Billy and James were so keen to please their mums that they agreed to sharpen all the tools, take baths and even do the shopping. Charlie offered to go too so that they could leave the baby dinosaurs outside SuperCave under the watchful eye of Steggy. SuperCave was Sabreton's biggest shop. It sold all sorts of things you never knew you needed. Charlie could think of better places to spend the day, but he wanted to help his friends keep their pets.

'Thanks for coming, Charlie,' said Billy. 'Steggy is a good influence on the twins.'

Charlie smiled weakly. 'Don't worry about it, it's not like we've got anything better to do. I've got to buy a new football, anyway.'

The boys had tried everything to stop Fing and Fang ruining their games, but nothing had worked. Every time they thought the baby dinosaurs had learnt to behave, one of them just couldn't resist scurrying on to the pitch and stealing their ball. In their excitement, they had burst every football the boys owned.

'I never knew having a pet dinosaur would be so

much trouble,' James grumbled. 'Last night Fing stole three sabre-tooth-tiger sausages from Mum's plate and then chewed through her chair leg. She toppled right on to the floor.'

Charlie giggled.

'Laugh all you like, Charlie Flint,' said James. 'But if Fing's behaviour doesn't improve by the time I go back to school on Monday, my mum says she'll do the same as Billy's mum and get rid of him!'

Billy picked up a nest of
pterodactyl eggs and put it
in his basket. A prim
looking lady in a pink and
purple SuperCave uniform
scurried over. She was Tanya
Trader, the shop's owner.

'They're buy one get one free,' she said, putting
another nest into Billy's basket. 'There are loads of great
offers in SuperCave if you know where to look. Let me
show you,' Tanya continued enthusiastically.

Before Billy could stop her, Tanya had grabbed him

by the arm and was leading
him around the shop plucking
things off the shelves.

'Nettles are three for two,'
she said putting three
bunches into Billy's basket.

'Mammoth milk is
half price, freshly squeezed berry juice is
on special offer, and have you tried this?'

Tanya held up a long green vegetable.

'What is it?' asked James,
wrinkling his nose.

'It's called a cucumber!' said Tanya

23

tossing it into Billy's basket. 'It's all the rage in Tuskville!'

'I don't care if they wear them like hats in Tuskville!' snapped Billy, taking the cucumber out of his basket and throwing it back on the shelf. 'I don't want it!'

'I was just trying to help,' said Tanya quietly.

Charlie saw that Tanya was upset and decided to smooth things over.

'Actually there is something we need . . .'

Tanya's eyes brightened. 'Anything!'

'Do you sell footballs?'

'SuperCave sells the best footballs in Sabreton!' said Tanya, happy again to be able to help.

She led the boys over to SuperCave's sports section. In among the whacking sticks, hunting spears and skipping vines was a box of sewn-hide footballs. While Charlie kept her busy with all sorts of questions, Billy and James finished the shopping in peace.

By the time Billy was ready to pay, Charlie knew everything there was to know about the footballs. Tanya had told him where they were made, what they were made from and how long they would last. She had even gone to school with the man who made the footballs. Charlie did his best to look interested and agreed to get two – the good thing about having a successful dinopants shop was that he wasn't short of precious stones to buy things with.

At the checkout, Billy unloaded his basket, while a bored-looking assistant kept count of everything he was buying.

'Fing and Fang seem to be behaving themselves for

once,' said Charlie, nodding towards the waiting dinosaurs.

'That's only because Steggy's there,' said Billy

loading up his rucksack. 'They love Steggy. As soon as he's gone they'll be as naughty as ever. They've got so much energy!'

Charlie's mind began to whirr. 'We need to tire Fing and Fang out,' he said. 'That way, at the end of the day, they won't be ready for mischief, they'll be ready for bed.'

Billy nodded. 'But we've taken them on walks. We went round T. Rex Mountain and back yesterday. I was exhausted, but they weren't. They need something really energetic!'

'It's a shame they can't play football with us,' said James chewing on a liquorice stick he'd just bought. 'They like that.'

'They're good at it too,' agreed Billy.

Charlie scratched his chin. Fing and Fang *were* pretty good at football. The only problem was that they always burst the ball.

'Are you collecting school vouchers?' asked the checkout assistant, holding up some yellow flower petals. 'They're for Mrs Heavystep – she wants a new pointing stick for the start of term.'

Billy nodded and shoved the vouchers in his rucksack. Maybe that would make up for Fing licking her.

'Why can't they play football with us?' said Charlie, as they packed their bags of shopping.

'Because they keep bursting the ball!' said Billy.

'It'd be too dangerous as well,' said James. 'They get

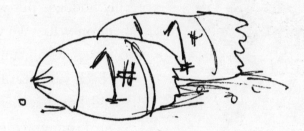

so carried away – we'd be flattened in no time!'

Suddenly, there was a commotion. The three boys turned just in time to see Fing and Fang hurtle past the shop door. They'd obviously got bored of waiting and were chasing each other up and down the street.

Billy rolled his eyes. 'I thought it was too good to last. We'd better sort this out.'

James nodded and raced for the door with Billy.

'I'll think of something,' called Charlie as the two boys ran from the shop. 'Trust me!'

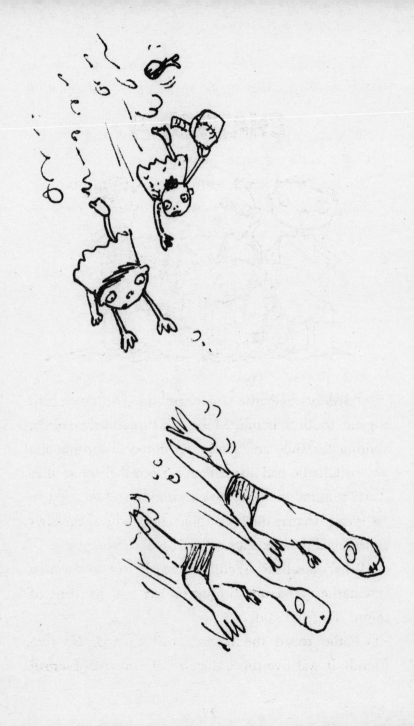

CHAPTER 4

Two days later, Charlie and Steggy were sitting next to a giant football beside Sabreton's dusty soccer pitch, waiting for Billy and James. School was starting that day, so Charlie had asked them to meet him just after dawn to show them his new invention.

'Ready to play dinoball?' giggled Charlie as the boys and their dinosaurs approached.

'What's *dino*ball?' asked Billy warily.

Charlie stood up and patted the ball in front of them. 'This,' he said.

Charlie rolled the massive ball towards his two friends. It was five times the size of a normal football and was made of extra thick mammoth-skin leather. James yelped as the heavy ball rolled over his foot.

'What do you think?' asked Charlie.

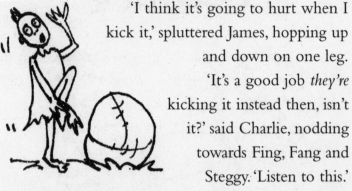

'I think it's going to hurt when I kick it,' spluttered James, hopping up and down on one leg.

'It's a good job *they're* kicking it instead then, isn't it?' said Charlie, nodding towards Fing, Fang and Steggy. 'Listen to this.'

Charlie knocked on the side of the football. It didn't sound full of air like a normal football, it sounded solid.

Billy smiled – that meant it wouldn't burst. Perhaps Charlie was on to something after all.

While Fing and Fang sniffed the ball curiously, Charlie explained all about his latest idea. He told them how he had asked Tanya Trader's school friend to make him a ball that was big and heavy enough to be used by dinosaurs. Tanya's friend had worked solidly all weekend and this ball was the result.

Billy giggled. 'This has to be your silliest idea yet. But if it stops Fang misbehaving I'll give it a go.'

'Me too!' agreed James.

Charlie rolled the dinoball towards the centre of the football pitch and began to explain to them how he thought the game should work.

'Dinoball is just like football, but for dinosaurs and humans,' he said.

'They'll trample us to pieces!' protested James.

'No, they won't,' explained Charlie. 'Because we sit on their backs. Steggy and I practised last night in the garden. You've got to make sure you hold on tight though – things can get pretty bumpy!'

Charlie clambered on to Steggy's back and showed the others. 'Now you try.'

Fing and Fang crouched down so that James and Billy could climb up. Billy gripped Fang around the neck while James held on to two of Fing's leathery scales. As soon as James was on Fing's back, the naughty dinosaur raced off around the football pitch bouncing him up and down.

'Ow!' cried James. 'He's bashing my bum!'

Charlie and Billy laughed as they watched Fing run in circles with James clinging on for dear life. When he got back to the centre circle, James climbed off and rubbed his bottom.

'I thought you said dinoball was going to be fun!'

'I had fun watching that!' said Billy, laughing.

Charlie suggested that the dinosaurs could kick the ball with their feet or head it, and they could also swipe it with their tail. The riders would help them spot opportunities and guide them round the pitch.

'Let's see how we get on,' suggested Charlie as he tapped Steggy softly between the shoulderblades. Steggy swiped the ball with his tail and in an instant Billy and Fang were racing after it.

'Woo-hoo!' yelped Billy as he cantered around the pitch. 'This is brilliant!'

Fing chased his brother. James clung on tight as they galloped towards the ball.

'What are we waiting for?' said Charlie, patting Steggy on the head. 'Let's get stuck in!'

Steggy didn't need to be asked twice and soon he and Charlie were charging around the pitch too.

In the early morning sun, Charlie, Billy and James headed, swiped and kicked the dinoball all around the dusty field. It was complete chaos! The dinosaurs had no idea about passing the ball to each other – they just whacked it!

It was so much fun they were all soon absorbed in playing and gradually they began to work out how to control the heavy ball. Fing and Fang were best when using their tails. James and Billy even found ways of telling them what to do next. They tapped them on the head if they wanted them to head the ball, on the bottom if they wanted them to use a tail-swipe and on the shoulders if they wanted their dinosaurs to kick.

Steggy and Charlie had been friends for so long that Steggy didn't need telling what to do. He instinctively knew what Charlie wanted and the pair chased round the football pitch as if they'd been playing dinoball all their lives.

Natalie Honeysuckle was on her way to school when she heard the commotion from the football pitch, and decided to investigate what was going on. She watched open-mouthed as Charlie and his friends hurtled around the pitch. It looked dangerous, but it also looked exciting, and if there was one thing Natalie loved more than anything else it was excitement.

She dropped her school bag on the dusty ground and ran towards the boys. 'That looks brilliant,' she called. 'Can I have a go?' 'You need a dinosaur to play dinoball,' said James as Fing swiped the ball towards his brother. Natalie looked at

Charlie hopefully. 'I could borrow Steggy?'

Charlie shook his head. Nobody rode Steggy but him. It was his one golden rule.

Natalie was about to turn and head for school when she spotted something moving in the bushes on the other side of the pitch – it was a baby maiasaura that was obviously also intrigued by the game. Natalie could tell by the look on its face that it was itching to join in just as much as she was. Suddenly Natalie had an idea – she delved into her school bag and took out the vine leaf wrap her mum had made for lunch. Then she crept around the pitch towards the curious dinosaur. When she got close, Natalie held out the vine leaf.

'I won't bite, I promise,' coaxed Natalie.

The maiasaura sniffed the wrap suspiciously. Then it licked its lips, stretched out a long black tongue and licked the wrap from top to bottom. Natalie tore off some pieces and laid a trail on the ground, luring the dinosaur out of the bushes.

Natalie patted it gently on the shoulder and then nodded towards the football pitch. The dinoball game was still going strong.

'Fancy a go?'

The dinosaur growled happily and crouched, nodding for Natalie to clamber on to its back.

As Natalie and her new dinosaur friend raced towards the dinoball, the three boys looked up in surprise.

'Well I never!' spluttered James. 'How did she do that?'

'Never underestimate Natalie Honeysuckle,' said Charlie, shaking his head with a rueful smile.

'Out of the way, boys!' cried Natalie. 'What are we playing anyway?'

'Dinoball!' shouted Charlie over the noise.

'Dinoball,' giggled Natalie. 'I like it!'

For the rest of the morning, the four children and their dinosaur friends raced up and down the pitch with glee. It was only when a furious Mrs Heavystep arrived to see why Charlie and his friends were late for their first day back at school that they stopped.

She was so angry with them that she gave them all a detention after school. They had to stay behind and polish a hundred flint spearheads each.

James and Billy were worried about what Fing and Fang might be getting up to without their supervision, but as they made their way home later that afternoon, the children found their dinosaur friends still happily kicking the ball back and forth on the pitch.

'I think this means they like it,' said Billy with a smile. 'And they are even behaving themselves too!'

'At last,' agreed James.

The friends watched as Fing and Fang skilfully batted the ball back and forth with their tails.

'I think you'll finally be getting some sleep tonight, too,' added Charlie.

Billy and James grinned at their friend.

'You are a total genius, Charlie Flint,' Billy said, patting him on the back.

CHAPTER 5

Charlie and his friends gathered each morning at the football pitch to play dinoball before school. Natalie had been thrilled to find that the baby maiasaura had returned, eager for another chance to play. After a few days, she thought it meant they were now friends, and decided to call her Mimi. They all enjoyed the games and, best of all, Fing and Fang were much better behaved after all their exercise.

'Shall we try playing a proper game today?' asked Billy on Thursday. 'One with teams and goals and everything?'

Charlie nodded. 'How about me and Natalie versus

you and James?' he suggested.

'You and your *girl*friend versus the two of us!' smirked James. 'Easy!'

'She's not my girlfriend!' protested Charlie, but nobody was listening.

The children mounted their dinosaurs and Charlie tapped Steggy on the shoulder to start the match.

To begin with everything went well. The dinosaurs passed the ball to each other nicely and nobody swiped or kicked it too hard. However, after Natalie and Mimi made a break down the wing to score a stunning goal, things started to go wrong. Fing and Fang wanted to get a goal themselves and they were so excited that Billy and James found it impossible to control them. In an effort to get the ball, Fing stamped on Steggy's tail. Steggy howled in pain.

'Foul!' cried Charlie. But Fing wasn't listening – he wanted to score a goal.

A small group of their schoolmates, attracted by the noise, had gathered at the side of the pitch to see what all the fuss was about. It wasn't long before they were caught up in the game and cheered as Fing hurtled towards the goal. The young dinosaur, egged on by their shouts and cries, turned and prepared to shoot a goal with his tail.

Natalie and Mimi rushed to stand on the goal line, and Fang ran to help his brother. Steggy tried to stop him, but Fang barged him out of the way, sending Charlie flying through the air! He landed on the ground with a thud. Angrily, Steggy grabbed Fang by his dinopants, pulling them down around his ankles. The dinopants tripped the baby dinosaur up and sent Billy tumbling too, much to the amusement of their schoolmates.

Meanwhile, Fing swiped the ball as hard as he could with his tail towards Natalie and Mimi, who were in goal. The dinoball flew towards the goal

with such force that Natalie was knocked right off her dinosaur and into the back of the goal.

The watching children were now rolling around, helpless with laughter.

Charlie had had enough. 'STOP!' he shouted.

The dinosaurs were so surprised, they halted in their tracks. As their school mates picked up their bags and headed towards first lesson, Charlie and his friends could hear their mocking laughter drifting away.

'That was terrible!' he said.

'We looked like a bunch of cave monkeys,' agreed James.

'I thought you'd be used to that by now!' muttered Billy under his breath.

James shot him an angry look.

'It was dangerous too,' said Natalie. 'Steggy got hurt, Charlie got hurt, Billy got hurt and I nearly had my head knocked off! If we're going to play dinoball properly, we need some proper dinoball rules.'

The others nodded in agreement.

'When Fing swiped the ball towards the goal with his tail, he wasn't even looking where it was going,' said Charlie.

'How could he?' protested James. 'He can't use his tail *and* watch the ball!'

'Exactly,' said Natalie. 'So we need a rule that says dinosaurs can only tail-swipe when they're kicking off – that way other players know what's going on and can keep a look out for flying dinoballs!'

'And *please* can we do something to stop my bum from hurting,' winced James, rubbing his bottom. 'All that bouncing can't be good for you.'

'And we'll need to find a safer way for humans to play so that they don't fall off all the time,' said Charlie.

'We could always use vine reins,' suggested Natalie. 'That's what farmers do when they ride their mammoths. For difficult dinosaurs, it would give us something to hold on to and help us control them too.'

Charlie said he'd go and see his farmer friend, Edward Arable, and find out exactly how it was done. 'Let's agree not to play another game of dinoball until we've worked out the rules properly,' he said.

'And can we *pleeease* find a way to stop my bottom hurting?' moaned James again.

'I'll think of something,' Charlie said, smiling as he punched his friend on the shoulder. 'Now we'd better hurry up or it'll be two hundred spearheads we'll have to polish if we're late again!'

Charlie and his friends spent their weekend coming up with ideas to help them play dinoball more safely.

Charlie visited Edward Arable to learn about vine reins. Natalie designed different pads stuffed with soft grass and moss that could be fixed into their their furskins, giving the rider a comfy seat. James was so relieved to hear about the idea that he and Billy worked extra hours in Charlie's dinopants shop to make them.

The rest of the time they practised their dinoball skills, and spent many hours working with their dinosaurs as a team, learning how to communicate better with each other, and practising passing and dribbling the ball.

Gradually word spread among the children of Sabreton that dinoball wasn't as dangerous or as silly as it had first appeared and some decided to give the game a second chance and watch the practice sessions. It wasn't just humans who liked dinoball either. Mimi had obviously been telling the young dinosaurs about it. Every morning, more and more dinosaurs of all shapes and sizes came along to the football field, keen to watch what was happening.

At the final training session of the week, the crowd had grown so large that Charlie encouraged his school friends to match themselves up with a dinosaur that wanted to play. Before he knew it, twelve pairs of dinosaurs and humans were on the pitch and knocking the dinoball back and forth.

Charlie smiled as he watched the excited dinoballers running around. It seemed like dinoball was going to be a great success.

CHAPTER 6

Deciding on the rules for dinoball proved to be much harder than Charlie expected. Everyone seemed to have their own ideas about how the game should be played. Some children thought that smaller dinosaurs should be allowed to tail-swipe if they wanted to, while others said that dinosaurs with spiky horns shouldn't be allowed on the pitch at all. Some said that dinosaurs that used four legs had an unfair advantage over those that used two.

'A dinoball goal should be three times as big as a football goal,' said Billy.

'No!' said Natalie. 'It should only be twice as big!'

After a lunchtime spent sitting at the log table, arguing about dinoball rules, they went back to their classroom to see Mrs Heavystep wearing her sports furskin and her hair tied back in a piece of bright yellow reed. It was games that afternoon and she liked to dress the part.

'Right!' she said, tapping her brand new pointing stick on the desk to get everybody's attention. 'Because you've all done so well in collecting your school vouchers from SuperCave . . .' Mrs Heavystep swished her new pointing stick proudly. '. . . this games lesson, I'm going to let you choose what game we play! So, who wants to play stickball?'

No one was very enthusiastic.

'Spear chucking?'

'We did that last week,' someone groaned.

'Oh well, I suppose you boys will want to play football,' she said with a sigh.

But no one sounded very enthusiastic about that either.

'Then what *do* you want to play?' asked Mrs Heavystep, leaning against the spear rack. She sounded as if she wished she'd never given them a choice.

'How about dinoball, Miss?' said Billy.

Mrs Heavystep looked confused. 'What's dinoball?' she asked. 'I've never heard of it.'

'It's a brilliant game that Charlie invented,' one boy began.

'Yeah – you sit on the back of dinosaurs,' said someone else.

Mrs Heavystep did not like the sound of that at all, especially since she remembered that Charlie and his friends had been late for school on the first day of term while doing something which sounded very similar to that.

'We'll show you!' said Natalie, heading for the door.

Mrs Heavystep was very reluctant to follow. Then again, Natalie Honeysuckle was such a sensible girl – and she *had* promised everyone they could choose what game they wanted to play.

While Charlie, James and Billy ran to round up their pet dinosaurs, Natalie led Mrs Heavystep and the rest of the class to the football pitch. The other dinosaurs only arrived at the pitch in the mornings when they knew there would be a practice, so it was left to Charlie, Billy and James to show how they played it with their dinosaurs, while Natalie and the rest of the class explained it to Mrs Heavystep.

'Well,' she said in the end. 'I've seen you practise, but how exactly do you play a match? What are the rules?'

'No one can agree on the rules,' explained Charlie. 'We tried to play a game once, but it ended in disaster.'

'I see,' said Mrs Heavystep, scratching her chin. 'Well, maybe I can help. Sometimes, when you can't agree on things, it's good to have an outside eye to help you decide what's what.'

For the rest of the afternoon, Mrs Heavystep and her class sat in the shade of a nearby tree while they tried to work out what the rules of dinoball should be.

There was a little bit of arguing of course, but by the time the mammoth horn sounded for the end of school, the children and Mrs Heavystep had come up

with the ten rules of dinoball. Mrs Heavystep asked Natalie to repeat them.

'Rule one: There are four human-dino pairs of players on each team.

'Rule two: Dinosaurs have to want to play the game – you can't force them.'

'And they can't be too big!' interrupted Billy.

Natalie fixed him with a fierce stare.

'I was just getting to that! Rule three: Dinosaurs

can't be too big. Any dinosaur that is much taller than the goalpost is not allowed to play.

'Rule four: Dinosaurs are allowed to hit the dinoball with their head, tail or foot. Nothing else is allowed.

'Rule five: Dinosaurs can only tail-swipe at kick-off, to save a goal, or when there's a goal kick.

'Rule six: There is to be no barging, pushing or biting. Players who persistently foul will be sent off. And that includes you, Billy Blackfoot!'

Billy gave an embarrassed smile. He already had a reputation for playing rough.

'Rule seven: We are going to have two referees, one

on each sideline. They'll watch from there so that they don't get hurt.'

'And I'm going to be one of them!' said Mrs Heavystep excitedly.

Natalie shot her a look. She didn't like all these interruptions.

'Oops! Sorry, Natalie,' Mrs Heavystep said, laughing.

The children giggled.

'Rule eight,' continued Natalie. 'Dinoball goals are to be thee times as big as football goals and a dinoball pitch is to be twice as long and twice as wide as a football pitch.

'Rule nine: The matches will last for as long as a football match.

'And most importantly, rule ten —'

'Have fun!' chorused the children in unison.

Mrs Heavystep smiled. 'Let's play our first match before school tomorrow,' she suggested. 'I'll find us a second referee if you draw out the pitch!'

That night the children worked long and hard

marking out the new dinoball pitch with small white stones in the light of flaming torches while Charlie, Billy and James made two huge goalposts using tough-looking vines and some extra long tree branches.

Once they were finished, the children promised to meet at the pitch the following morning.

Lying in bed that night, Charlie didn't get a wink of sleep. The thought of finally playing a proper game of dinoball made his heart pound with excitement. But would everything work out as they had planned?

CHAPTER 7

Mrs Heavystep was waiting for the children by the new dinoball pitch when they arrived the following morning.

'Chop! Chop!' said Mrs Heavystep, clapping her hands. 'We haven't got all day! The other referee and I have been ready for ages!'

'Who *is* the other referee, Miss?' asked Charlie.

Boris, the mayor of Sabreton's burly bodyguard, stepped out from behind a tree and tooted his little wooden trumpet proudly. He usually only used the trumpet to announce the mayor's arrival, but he didn't see why he couldn't use it in dinoball matches as well.

'Do you have a spare one of those?' asked Mrs Heavystep.

Boris fished inside his pocket and produced a second trumpet, which he handed to Mrs Heavystep.

'If anyone breaks the rules, one of us will blow our trumpet. If that happens, you're to stop playing and await further instructions.'

The children nodded. They didn't think there'd be much rule breaking with Boris and Mrs Heaystep on patrol.

There were sixteen dinosaurs and sixteen children in all so Mrs Heavystep picked out four teams of four. While two of the teams played each other, the other two teams watched. After the first match, Mrs Heavystep swapped them over.

Charlie, Natalie, Billy and James made up one team to start with. Because they had been playing for longer than anyone else, they were much better, and so it wasn't long before Mrs Heavysteap mixed the teams up so Charlie and his friends were captain of one team each. The matches became far more even, and more exciting too!

The four teams played each other while the sun rose in the sky and Mrs Heavystep and Boris trotted up and down the sidelines watching for fouls.

The new rules worked brilliantly, and by the time they had to stop to go to school, no rider or dinosaur had been hurt.

Mrs Heavystep and Boris had enjoyed themselves so much that they volunteered to referee for the children every morning before school and early morning dinoball sessions were soon a regular part of the day.

Mrs Heavystep was, much to everyone's surprise, a huge fan of dinoball, and even paid to have some spare dinoballs made for practice with the school's money, claiming it promoted teamwork. When they weren't playing matches against each other, Mrs Heavystep

helped the children and their dinosaurs to improve their skills.

The dinosaurs would practise tail-swipes, then play keepie-uppie with their heads to make their necks nice and strong. Once they had finished doing that, Mrs Heavystep would place six large rocks in a line across the playground and the dinosaurs and children  would have to take it in turns to weave in and out of them, dribbling the heavy dinoball or football as they went. By far the hardest skill was dino-control. The children had to learn how to make the dinosaurs do what they were told by tapping their dinosaur or tugging on their vine ropes so that the dinosaurs would understand what they wanted them to do.

Everyone played hard and had fun, but was also totally exhausted after the training sessions and games. Even Fing and Fang were so busy practising that they were too tired to cause any trouble at home and Mrs Tusk and Mrs Boulder both agreed that Billy and James could keep them for as long as they wanted.

Dinoball fast became the latest craze to sweep Sabreton

School. Everyone reckoned it was more fun than apricot stone marbles, more interesting than beetle racing and more exciting than sabre-tooth-tiger tag.

When they weren't playing or watching dinoball, they all liked to discuss it. They each had an opinion as to which type of dinosaur made the best player. Some believed that small dinosaurs were best as they could sprint up the wing past the big dinosaurs and score lots of goals. Some thought that dinosaurs with big teeth or sharp horns were best because they  could scare the opposition. Billy thought that you needed a large dinosaur to play properly because they could hit the ball harder than any of the others. Charlie  thought that the perfect dinoball team would include different dinosaurs – you needed a speedy dinosaur to score but you also needed strong and scary ones to help them do that. Many a happy lunchtime was spent discussing tactics.

Mrs Heavystep even organised a school dinoball league. Every weekend, the four school teams would play each other on the dinoball pitch. By the end of the first session a small group of parents had gathered to watch – it had been so quiet in the town that some of them had wondered where all the children were. At first, they didn't know what to make of the game, but it wasn't long before they too got swept up in the craze and were cheering with delight.

Every week the crowd seemed to get a little larger, and it soon seemed like every adult in Sabreton was at the dinoball pitch watching the children and dinosaurs play. Dinosaurs came too, to growl and hiss encouragement to their friends. Peter Tray started bringing vine-leaf wraps and bottles of his special

punch to sell to hungry dinoball supporters as they cheered from the sidelines.

Everyone agreed that dinoball was a brilliant game. It gave the children – and dinosaurs – lots of exercise and plenty of fresh air and it was also very exciting to watch.

★   ★   ★

One day, after a particularly exhausting match, Tanya Trader, the owner of SuperCave, ran over to Charlie. Charlie rolled his eyes – the last thing he needed after a game of dinoball was Tanya Trader telling him about her latest special offers. He tried his best to be polite.

'Dinoball is so exciting!' she gushed.

'Everyone loves it,' he agreed. 'Thanks for persuading your friend to make the first ever dinoball. Without him the game would never have got started.'

Tanya beamed from ear to ear. 'That's what I wanted to tell you,' she said. 'My friend says he's been getting lots of orders for dinoballs recently.'

'Really?' said Charlie, scratching his head. 'Who from? We haven't asked for any more.'

'The orders aren't coming from Sabreton – they're coming from schools as far away as Fangbury, Tuskville and Talontree! It looks like your dinoball game is spreading across the country!'

Charlie gasped in surprise – and so did his friends when he told them.

'I wonder if these other schools are any good?' said Natalie.

'They couldn't be as good as us!' boasted James.

'We'd need to play them to find out for sure,' said Natalie, smiling mischieviously.

Charlie's eyes lit up. 'What a good idea!' he said. 'That's exactly what we should do! I'm going to see the mayor!'

CHAPTER 8

Leslie Trumpbottom, the mayor of Sabreton, was a short man with a thick black moustache. He was the most important man there, and if you wanted to do anything that affected the town, you needed to ask his permission first. His office walls were adorned with the finest cave paintings and a beautiful sabre-tooth-tiger-skin rug covered the floor. On quiet days, when no one was watching, he liked to scrunch his toes in the soft, fuzzy fur of the rug and hum a little song. This was exactly what he was doing when Boris, his bodyguard, burst in, with Charlie close behind.

'Haven't you heard of knocking?' spluttered the

mayor, straightening his robes. 'I'm very busy!'

Boris and Charlie exchanged glances. The mayor didn't look very busy.

'Thanks for seeing me, Mr Mayor!' gabbled Charlie. 'I've just been playing dinoball. Have you heard of it? Of course you have! Anyway, I've found out that it's being played all over the country and I thought —'

The mayor held up his hands for silence and pointed to the chair in front of his desk.

'Calm down, Charlie! I can't understand a word you're saying. Take a seat and start again.'

Charlie blushed and sat down. 'Sorry, Mr Mayor, I'm a bit excited.'

'So I can see,' the mayor said, smiling.

'I've had an idea,' began Charlie.

The mayor pulled at his moustache. Charlie's ideas were usually very good – he'd come up with dinopants and dinoloos after all. The only invention that had been a disaster was the terrible drink that Charlie had created that had made all the dinosaurs burp non-stop. The mayor had done his best to forget about that.

'It's about dinoball,' said Charlie.

'Ah yes,' said the mayor, nodding. 'I haven't had the chance to watch a match myself but it seems to be very popular. If I'm not mistaken, Boris has something to do with it.'

'He's one of our referees,' said Charlie.

'A very good choice,' replied the mayor. 'If he's tough enough to be my bodyguard then he's tough enough to look after a game of dinoball!' Boris smiled and stared sheepishly at the floor.

'And who's the other referee?' asked the mayor.

'Mrs Heavystep,' answered Charlie.

The colour drained from the

mayor's face as he remembered long days spent in Sabreton School trying not to get on the wrong side of his formidable teacher.

'Another good choice,' he gulped. 'There's no one in Sabreton scarier than her!'

Charlie giggled and told the mayor what he had learnt from Tanya about the other schools playing dinoball.

'This is all very interesting, Charlie,' said the mayor, 'but it still doesn't explain why you're here.'

Charlie began to tell the mayor all about his big idea. 'I want Sabreton to hold a dinoball tournament,' he said. 'We can invite the top team from schools in other towns to come and play the top team from Sabreton.'

'And which is the top team in Sabreton?' asked the

mayor. 'Aren't there four of them?'

'We could hold official dinoball trials,' said Charlie, thinking on his feet. 'That way we can be sure to find the best players.'

The mayor stroked his chin. The idea sounded interesting, but there were a few practical problems he would have to consider. 'Where would the teams stay?' he asked.

'Everybody could camp beside the dinoball pitch,' said Charlie.

The mayor nodded. It would be good for the children of different towns to meet each other. 'But wouldn't it be very disruptive?' he said, twirling his moustache around his finger. 'Nothing would get done because everybody would want to watch the matches!'

Charlie thought again. 'We could hold the championship over a weekend. And the town would be full of people. Think how good that would be for all the shops and cafés. They'd be packed!'

The mayor's eyes lit up. That decided the matter. Full shops and cafés were a very good thing indeed. 'Let's do it!' he said, clapping his hands in excitement. 'We've no time to waste. If we want a dinoball tournament we need to get cracking!'

The mayor turned to his bodyguard. 'Boris!'

Boris saluted.

'Go and fetch Andy Leggit! He must take a message to the schools in Talontree, Fangbury and Tuskville inviting them all to bring their best dinoball teams to a dinoball tournament here in Sabreton the weekend after next!'

Charlie smiled and hurried back to the dinoball pitch to tell his friends the wonderful news.

CHAPTER 9

From then on, Sabreton was buzzing with talk of the forthcoming dinoball tournament. Andy Leggit had returned with messages of acceptance from all the schools and Mrs Heavystep cancelled the weekend's dinoball matches to hold trials for the official Sabreton dinoball team.

The mayor had also announced there would be a town vote to decide on a name for the new Sabreton team. He reckoned the best suggestions were the Sabreton Sprinters, the Sabreton Sureshots (which had been Billy's suggestion) and the Sabreton Tail-swipes. He placed a large stone container in the centre of the town square and people voted for their favourite name by putting in black, brown or white stones depending on their choice. The name of the team was to be revealed at the dinoball trials.

When the day of the trials arrived, eight dinosaurs and eight children stood on the dinoball pitch waiting for Mrs Heavystep to arrive, and there was a large crowd to cheer them on. There were more who would have loved to be in the team, but only those who thought they had a really good chance of being selected put themselves forward.

When Mrs Heavystep finally marched into the centre circle, everyone fell silent. You could have cut the atmosphere with a slicing stone.

'Welcome to the first ever dinoball trials,' she announced. 'These children are here to compete against each other for a place in the official Sabreton dinoball team, the name of which will be revealed once we have finished.'

Charlie's heart was beating like a drum as he stroked Steggy nervously.

'As you know, only four pairs of dinosaurs and children can be on the team and we have come up with five trials to help us decide which we should pick. So, let the trials begin!'

Mrs Heavystep tooted on her trumpet and beckoned the children and dinosaurs forward.

'The first trial is a running race,' she explained. 'From the centre circle to the far goal and back again. OK?'

The children nodded and the eight pairs lined up. Mrs Heavystep cleared her throat. 'On your marks, get set, go!'

A cheer went up from the crowd as the dinosaurs thundered down the pitch. Natalie and Mimi took an early lead, with Charlie and Steggy close behind, while James and Billy were bringing up the rear on Fing and Fang. As the dinosaurs turned to race back to the centre circle, one of Charlie's classmates, Leo Bucket, overtook him on a speedy bagaceratops he called Spud. Leo had been getting better and better at dinoball and Charlie knew he was a real contender for the team.

As they hurtled across the line it was Natalie in first place with Leo in second and Charlie in third. Billy was last.

'Oh no!' moaned Billy, as they all lined up for the second trial. 'I'm never going to be on the team if I come last!'

'Don't be so hard on yourself,' whispered Natalie. 'We need all sorts of players in the team. You could always be a goalie. You don't need to move so fast for that.'

* * *

For the rest of the morning the crowd watched as Mrs Heavystep put the children and their dinosaurs through their paces. Trial two showed off their dribbling skills and trial three demonstrated their passing. Trial four was all about being in goal. By the final trial, there were only six pairs left on the pitch. One dinosaur had pulled out with an injury and one caveboy had fallen off his dinosaur and hurt his arm. The six remaining players looked at each other fiercely. They were Charlie and his three friends, Leo Bucket and a boy called Tommy Nettles who rode a gallimimus, called Gally, with a really long tail.

'The final trial is goal scoring!' announced Mrs Heavystep.

Charlie was looking forward to this – it was what he and Steggy were best at.

One by one the children lined up in front of the goalmouth and took it in turns to fire the ball into

the goal. Natalie, Billy, Leo and James all scored with ease, piling the pressure on Charlie. But he needn't have worried – Steggy slammed the ball with his front foot and the ball thumped into the goal. Charlie whooped with delight and gave Steggy a well-done scratch.

The last player to kick was Tommy Nettles. Gally thwacked the ball so hard it sailed over the top of the goal. Tommy shook his head in disbelief.

Once the trials were over, Mrs Heavystep and Boris retreated to discuss who of the six remaining contenders would be in the final team. When they returned, Boris blew on his trumpet to stop the chattering and Mrs Heavystep began to speak.

'After a very tightly fought morning of trials, we are pleased to announce that the four pairs of players who have made it on to the Sabreton dinoball team are, in no particular order . . .' Mrs Heavystep paused

dramatically. 'Natalie Honeysuckle and Mimi . . .'
Natalie gave a cheer and kissed Mimi on the
cheek. 'James Tusk and Fing . . .'
James punched the air and patted
Fing on the back. 'Charlie Flint
and Steggy . . .' Charlie waved
to his dad who gave him two
thumbs up. 'And finally . . .'
Leo, Billy and Tommy held their
breath. It was between the three
of them. '. . . Leo Bucket and
Spud.'

While Leo and Spud
celebrated, Charlie ran over to
give Billy a hug. 'I'm sorry,
Billy,' he whispered. 'I thought
you did very well.'

Billy was too upset to reply.

'It was very difficult to choose a team from the six
remaining pairs,' continued Mrs Heavystep, 'but we felt
that two allosauruses on one team wouldn't give us the
variety we needed to win and it's vital to have a reliable
goal scorer, so Tommy and Gally, and Billy and Fang are
to be reserve players.'

Leo Bucket offered his hand to Billy. 'No hard
feelings?' he said.

'No hard feelings,' said Billy with a sad smile.

The mayor made his way into the centre of the pitch. 'It is with great pleasure that I can announce that the name you have decided to give the new Sabreton dinoball team is . . . the Sabreton Sureshots!'

The crowd cheered and Natalie looked at Billy, smiling. 'Your team name got chosen! That's forever. The team will still be called the Sabreton Sureshots long after the rest of us are too old to play!'

Billy smiled weakly back at her. It did make him feel a little bit better.

'And as a special surprise,' continued the mayor, 'I can also unveil the new team kit.'

Charlie looked up – he hadn't been expecting a team kit.

Tanya Trader made her way on to the pitch holding a mysterious looking box. 'The Sabreton Sureshots are going to be sponsored by SuperCave,' she announced.

'Which means they will be playing in the store colours.'

Charlie gulped. He had a bad feeling about this. Tanya reached into the box and pulled out pink and purple tunics for all the players.

'You know,' sniggered Billy as the rest of the team examined their new kit, 'I'm not so sad about being left off the team now. At least I won't have to wear that horrible thing in front of the whole town!'

Charlie, Natalie, Leo and looked at each other and laughed. The big caveboy had a point.

CHAPTER 10

Mrs Heavystep and Boris made the Sabreton Sureshots train every day before and after school. It was decided that Fing and James would be in goal, Leo and Spud would be defenders, Natalie and Mimi would be in the middle of the pitch and Charlie and Steggy would be the goal strikers. Because Charlie and Steggy had known each other for so long, they could react quicker than anybody else when the ball flew their way. This, explained Mrs Heavystep, was vital if the team wanted to make the most of their goal scoring opportunities.

While the Sureshots practised their skills on the pitch, the rest of the town got ready for the tournament. The mayor had organised four big tents to be put up in a field next to the dinoball pitch. He'd also managed to find a valuable-looking beaker in a back room at Sabreton Museum to use as a prize, and so the dinoball tournament became known as the Dinoball Cup.

Peter Tray stayed up late making vine leaf wraps and bucket-loads of his special punch, while Tanya Trader ordered hundreds of replica kits so that Sureshot supporters could wear the team colours as they cheered them on. She also managed to find some special shells that made a honking sound when you blew into them. She knew they would be perfect for encouraging the players on the pitch and put them on special offer at the front of her shop.

By the end of the week, Sabreton was even more dinoball crazy than it had been before. Scraps of animal hide painted in the team colours hung from the trees, and nearly everyone in the town seemed to be clutching one of Tanya's honking shells. Johnny Herb, the town's medicine man who always spoke in rhyme, even came up with a song that the supporters could sing to cheer on the team when they weren't honking their shells. He tried to teach anyone who would listen:

'Sabreton Sureshots! Go, team, go!
You will win come rain or snow!
You are better than all the rest!
Sabreton Sureshots, you're
the best!'

Before the team knew it, it was the evening before the start of the Dinoball Cup. Charlie and his friends were sitting nervously in The Hungry Bone Café, ready to welcome the arriving teams and point them in the direction of the tents.

The first person to come running up the High Street was a very athletic-looking man.

'Jim Hawk,' said the man, bobbing up and down on his feet. 'Headteacher of Talontree school and coach of the Talontree Tornadoes.'

He spoke very quickly, like he was out of breath.

'We ran all the way here,' said Jim, nodding to a group of children in blue and yellow kits, who were jogging on the spot a short distance away.

'All the way!' gasped Natalie. 'But that must have taken ages!'

Jim nodded as he bent down to touch his toes. 'A fit dinoball team is a winning dinoball team, that's my motto!'

Charlie looked at the children exercising. He didn't fancy his chances against any of them in a running race.

'Why didn't you ride your dinosaurs?' asked Leo Bucket.

Jim stopped stretching and looked at the caveboy in shock. 'A dinoball dinosaur is a prime athlete!' he spluttered. 'They're not to be used for riding around the country willy nilly. Besides, if we'd ridden all the way here we wouldn't have got any exercise, would we, and a fit dinoball team is a winning dinoball team!'

'So you said,' muttered Charlie.

The dinosaurs on the Talontree team were slurping water from the pond. Charlie noticed that every dinosaur had been clearly chosen for speed, and moved on two legs rather than four. Charlie spotted a dryosaurus, an iguanodon and two ornithomimuses.

'I see you're sussing out our strikers,' said Jim, swinging his arms above his head.

'You've got *two* strikers?' said Natalie, her eyes wide. 'We've only got one.'

'Well, I hope he's fast!' said Jim, beginning to jog

once again. 'Now where do we have to go?'

Charlie pointed up the hill towards the campsite. 'Turn left when you get to the dinoball pitch. There's a tent there for you. You'll need a rest after your long trip.'

'Nonsense!' spat Jim as he turned and sprinted back towards his team. 'We've still got more training to do! Come on you, lazy lumps! Let's get moving! No time for slacking! Pick your knees up!'

Obediently the Talontree Tornadoes trotted up the hill towards the campsite.

'Wow!' said Leo after they'd gone.

'My thoughts exactly,' mumbled James. 'We don't stand a chance against them!'

Charlie shook his head. 'Don't be so sure. They may look fast and fit but they don't look strong. There's no dinosaur like Fing or Steggy to give them power and muscle behind hitting the ball.'

Before Charlie had a chance to sit down, another

stranger ambled into town on the back of a diplodocus. He couldn't have been more different to Jim Hawk – he had a big bushy beard and a mass of shaggy red hair. His clothes looked like he'd patched them together out of different furskins.

'I'm Clive Spittle,' said the man, wiping his hand on his furskin before offering it to each of the Sabreton Sureshots in turn. 'Coach of the Fangbury Flyers.'

Clive spoke with a long slow drawl. Every word seemed to take forever to leave his mouth. He nodded up the high street to where his team were lolloping into town. They were all riding triceratopses and didn't look much like flyers.

'It's more a name than a description,' said Clive, as if he was reading their thoughts. 'Nothing really flies in Fangbury. Where do you want us to go?'

'There's a tent for you up the hill,' said Charlie.

'A tent!' gasped Clive, his eyes wide. 'How fancy!'

Clive called to his team. 'Come on, you lot! We've got a tent! We'll be living a life of luxury here in Sabreton!'

The rest of the Fangbury Flyers murmured appreciatively as they turned and made their way to the campsite.

'Now that's more like it,' said Leo with a smile. 'We'll beat them easily.'

'We can't take anything for granted,' Charlie said, though he was quite relieved too. 'Those triceratopses may not move fast, but they're big and they'll block the ball. They could cause trouble just by getting in the way.'

The last team to arrive in Sabreton were the

Tuskville Terrors. They were wearing yellow and white furskins and were sitting on the backs of their dinosaurs. Charlie introduced himself.

'How super!' gushed their coach with a bow, as he got off his dinosaur and shook Charlie's hand. 'I'm Cuthbert Polish, and these are the Tuskville Terrors. Don't be put off by the name, we're not that terrible!' Cuthbert threw his head back and laughed. 'Well, isn't this quaint!' he said, putting his hands on his hips and looking around. 'I haven't seen a town like this in years. I didn't know they still existed. When you live in Tuskville you get used to things being a little bit more modern.' Cuthbert laughed loudly once again. 'I am so sorry we're late.

Took us ages to get here. We had to stop for lunch by a horrid, stinky bog on the far side of that mountain.' Cuthbert pointed at T. Rex mountain. 'That would be the Bog of Ooze,' explained Charlie. 'You're lucky you didn't get stuck.'

Cuthbert chuckled. 'It would take more than a squelchy old bog to catch out someone from Tuskville! Would you like a cherry?'

Charlie shook his head.

'Suit yourself,' said Cuthbert, popping it in his mouth. 'I can't get enough of them!' As he chewed, Cuthbert looked James up and down and spat out the cherry stone. 'How super!' he giggled. 'You're still wearing an old-fashioned jaguar furskin!'

James was rather proud of his clothes, and he looked furious.

'And you're all barefoot! Don't you have any of these?'

Cuthbert lifted his foot up for the others to see.

There were small pieces of leather tied on to his feet with straps.

'They're called shoes,' he explained. 'They'll catch on here eventually, I'm sure!'

Cuthbert laughed once again. It was starting to get on Charlie's nerves.

'Now,' said Cuthbert, clapping his hands together importantly. 'I'd love to stay and chat but we've come a very long way and we need to get ready for the match. Where are we staying?'

Charlie pointed up the hill.

'The tent's up there, just next to the dinoball pitch,' said James.

'A tent! How super!' chuckled Cuthbert. 'Don't worry, though — we've brought our own. It's made from sabre-tooth-tiger fur, you know. It cost me quite a few precious stones, but they're all the rage in Tuskville! Our star striker Craig Shredder won't sleep in anything less.' Cuthbert pointed to the largest boy in his team who was riding a giant velociraptor. Both boy and dinosaur glared at Charlie.

As Cuthbert and his team marched off, Charlie noticed that the rest of the Terrors were riding large, meat-eating dinosaurs too. As well as the velociraptor he spotted a saltopus and an oviraptor. Not many

people could afford to keep those sorts of dinosaur –
they ate so much meat.

'Well, they're a bit posh! How *suuuuper*!' mocked
James.

Charlie grinned. 'Don't be so rude! Besides, we need
to go and practise if we want to win the Dinoball
Cup!'

His team-mates cheered, finished their drinks and
made their way to their tent, singing the Sureshot song
at the top of their voices.

CHAPTER 11

After an early night and a hearty breakfast made by Peter Tray, all the teams got ready for the first two matches of the Dinoball Cup. Mrs Heavystep met with the coaches to decide the order of play. There were to be two games on day one with the winners of those matches playing each other the following day in the final. Mrs Heavystep held out four pieces of straw, two of which were painted red at the bottom. The coaches picked one straw each. The teams of those who picked the painted straws were to play each other first, after which the remaining two teams would play.

The first match was the Sabreton Sureshots against

the Talontree Tornadoes. Kick off was when the sun rose above the third tree on the horizon. Then the Tuskville Terrors would take on the Fangbury Flyers.

'How super!' said Cuthbert. 'May I suggest the coaches of the two teams not playing act as referees?'

The other teachers nodded. That sounded fair enough.

As Charlie and his team-mates prepared for the match, they watched the crowd swell. A group of supporters from Talontree jogged into town. They looked just as sporty as the Talontree players and had painted their faces in blue and yellow to match their team's colours.

'How cool do they look?' gasped Leo.

Charlie had to admit that the Talontree supporters did look pretty cool.

Mrs Heavystep and the mayor strode into the centre of the pitch and nodded for silence. When Mrs Heavystep announced which teams would be playing first, a murmur of excitement rippled through the crowd. Charlie gulped and looked over to the Talontree team. They had made their dinosaurs blue dinopants with a yellow lightning bolt stitched on the bum.

As the Tornadoes took their positions on the pitch, Mrs Heavystep called her team close. 'Listen all of you!' she said. 'Play hard, play fair and do your best!'

Charlie and the rest of the team nodded, mounted their dinosaurs and strode into the centre of the pitch. The crowd cheered loudly when they saw the home team. Charlie allowed himself a little smile. He felt proud and nervous at the same time. He could see his mum and dad in the crowd.

His dad waved and shouted. 'Go, Charlie! Go, Sureshots!'

Cuthbert Polish and Clive Spittle ran to the sidelines to act as referees. Cuthbert tooted on his trumpet and the game began.

The Talontree Tornadoes were well trained and immediately began to nip up and down the pitch. Before James had even realised they'd kicked off, a skinny young boy on the back of a ornithomimus was lining up a shot on goal. Fing growled at him and tried to fill as much of the goalmouth as possible, but the ornithomimus wasn't intimidated – he struck the ball with his foot. There wasn't much power in the shot, though, and Fing was able to save it easily with a swipe of his tail, but it was clear the Sureshots couldn't let their concentration slip for a moment.

'They're fast, aren't they?' muttered Natalie, as she and Leo tried to keep up with the opposition.

'Really fast,' agreed Leo, 'but I don't think their strikers are up to much.'

Leo was proved right. Time after time, the Tornadoes shot at goal, but the strikers didn't have the power they needed and Fing was always able to save it. But the Tornadoes were also fast when it came to defending and the Sureshots hadn't had any shots at goal. By half-time the score was nil-nil.

'This is impossible!' huffed Charlie as he slumped to the ground. 'I haven't had one decent shot.'

'Sorry, Charlie,' said Leo. 'We've been so busy defending, we haven't been able to get the ball to you.'

'I'm not blaming you,' Charlie told him. 'They're just so fast!'

The other children nodded in agreement.

Billy came up to them. 'I've been watching closely. They're so nippy that they all zoom after the ball together rather than stay in formation. They can't keep that up for the whole match – they'll tire themselves out. When that happens, lure them all up to our end of the pitch and get the ball to Charlie. They'll be so exhausted they won't have time to sprint back and defend.'

'That's brilliant!' said Charlie. 'We'll give it a try.'

The second half was a completely different story. The Tornadoes still zipped all over the field but rather than worry about it, the Sureshots made sure the Tornadoes tired themselves out. When the Tornadoes started to slow down, Natalie and Mimi dribbled the

95

ball towards the Sureshots' goal. Just like Billy said, the whole Tornado team chased after it. At the last possible moment, Mimi hoofed the ball over their heads to land at Steggy's feet. Steggy was on top of it in a second, and with a mighty thump Steggy walloped the ball between the goal posts.

The crowd roared and honked their shells with excitement. It was one-nil to Sabreton!

Having scored one goal, Charlie and Steggy were a lot more confident. Because Steggy hadn't had much to do in the first half he still had loads of energy left. He and Charlie darted up and down the pitch, carving out chance after chance. It wasn't long until Leo and Spud managed to dribble the ball past the Tornadoes' defence and Steggy was on it in an instant. He danced towards the goalkeeper, guiding the ball this way and that. The crowd on the sidelines had never seen such skill from a dinosaur before. It was as if the ball was stuck to Steggy's foot. With a grunt, Steggy fired the ball through the goalkeeper's legs and made it two-nil.

As the final minutes of the game played out, Steggy was determined to score a hat trick. Charlie guided him to dribble the ball from his own goal line past every player on the Tornadoes team. He was making it look easy and the Tornadoes were too tired to do anything about it. Steggy teased the players with his skill and then fired a shot into the goal with the back of his head and it was three-nil just as the final trumpet sounded. The Sureshots were through to the final!

Charlie ran to give Billy a thank you hug.

'Don't get too carried away,' Billy said, laughing. 'You've still got one more game to play!'

Charlie didn't care. For the moment, he basked in the noise of the wildly cheering crowd with his grinning team-mates. They were simply going to enjoy the victory.

CHAPTER 12

After Peter Tray had sold out of vine leaf wraps at lunchtime, the crowd reassembled for the second match of the day. The Tornadoes and the Sureshots settled down with beakers of punch to watch the game together. The Tuskville Terrors marched on to the pitch in their white and yellow dinoball kits with their heads held high. Their dinosaurs looked fearsome and ready for anything. In contrast, the Fangbury Flyers wore a kit made out of rough reeds beautifully woven together and tied with a simple vine belt, and their dinosaurs looked half asleep. The Tuskville team sniggered as they watched the others amble on to the pitch. As far as

Cuthbert Polish was concerned, his team had already won.

Just as the teams were taking their postions, a group of triceratopses pulling large carts made its way up the hill to the pitch. The carts were full of people wearing indentical reed outfits.

'Not too late, are we?' drawled a voice from the cart. 'We're the Fangbury Flyers' supporters club. Took a bit longer than we thought to get here!'

Mrs Heavystep delayed the opening tail-swipe while the Fangbury supporters found a place in the crowd.

As the match began, Charlie and his friends had as much fun watching the Fangbury supporters as the game. Whenever they got excited they would yell and wave strips of woven reed scarves in the air.

'We'll have to get some of those!' Charlie said to his friends.

The match was much closer than anyone had thought it would be. It didn't seem like the Flyers had any tactics at all, but their big lumbering triceratopses meant that they were always in the way of the Tuskville team. No matter what the Terrors tried to do, they always found a Fangbury dinosaur blocking them. The Terrors may have had muscular, well-fed dinosaurs, but if they couldn't get past the triceratopses then they weren't much use at all.

On the sideline, Cuthbert Polish was getting angrier and angrier.  He shouted instructions to his team. His star player, Craig Shredder, was getting more and more impatient, and the more impatient he got, the more he and his velociraptor, Spitball, tried to cheat.

'I don't like the way they're acting. Someone's going to get hurt,' said Natalie, shaking her head as she watched Craig and Spitball trample up and down the pitch.

Charlie had to agree. By half-time the score was still

nil-nil and Craig was fuming. He shouted at his team as they left the pitch, blaming everyone else for the lack of goals.

When the match resumed, the Terrors were getting so frustrated by the Flyers that they started to make mistakes. One of the Fangbury Flyers found himself next to an open goal and while their supporters waved their scarves in the air, the lumbering dinosaur nudged the ball through the posts for the first goal.

Cuthbert Polish shrieked instructions louder than ever. After play resumed, Craig checked over his shoulders to make sure the referees couldn't see, and then, right under Charlie and his friends' noses, he barged Spitball straight into one of the Fangbury triceratopses, sending its rider flying.

'Did you see that?' hissed Natalie. 'What a cheat!'

Mrs Heavystep turned to look just as the Fangbury player pulled himself to his feet and angrily tried to yank Craig off Spitball. Mrs Heavystep, having missed the first foul, sent the Fangbury player and his Triceratops off the pitch in disgrace. Craig gave Charlie and his friends a sly grin. Charlie bristled. He couldn't stand cheats.

'How super!' yelled Cuthbert from the sidelines. Now that the Fangbury Flyers were down to three men, his team had a chance.

The Tuskville Terrors wasted no time in taking advantage of their extra man and soon the score was even. Shortly after that, Craig and Spitball powered down the touchline to score the winning goal and the final trumpet blew.

'What a rotten bunch,' grumbled James as the Terrors soaked up the applause. 'They don't deserve to be in the final at all!'

'At least *we* know they play dirty,' agreed Charlie.

'I can't believe Mrs Heavystep got it so wrong!' said Leo, shaking his head.

'I reckon that's how they work,' said Billy, coming over. 'They foul the other team when no one's looking, and get them angry enough to try a foul back.'

'When we play them tomorrow we have to make sure we don't get angry,' said Leo. 'That's what they want.'

Charlie nodded. This was good advice. He'd have to make sure he, Steggy and the rest of the Sureshots kept their cool when it came to the final, no matter what the Tuskville Terrors threw at them.

'And you'll need to score more goals, Charlie,' added James. 'They focus on the attack, so it should leave their

half of the pitch open for you and Steggy to score whenever we can get the ball to you.'

Charlie bit his lip. He and Steggy would have to put in another brilliant performance the following day. Could they do it two games in a row?

That night, the Sureshots, the Flyers and the Tornadoes all sat around a campfire eating mammoth meat sausages. The children had heard all about Charlie Flint and his dinopants and Charlie kept them laughing as he told them all about his adventures.

The only team that didn't join in the fun were the

Tuskville Terrors. Cuthbert had made it clear they weren't interested. 'No hard feelings, old chaps,' he'd said, 'but we need a good night's sleep to make sure we win the cup tomorrow.'

The other children soon began to feel sleepy themselves. Before he went to bed, Charlie checked on Steggy, who was sleeping around the back of the tents with all the other dinosaurs. 'Sleep well, Steggy,' he said. 'It's a really important day tomorrow, but I know you'll be brilliant.'

Steggy snorted contentedly in his sleep, and it wasn't long until the campsite rang to the noise of snoring children and dinosaurs.

CHAPTER 13

The following morning, the Sureshots were up bright and early.

'Today's the day we get to show those Terrors what we're made of,' said Leo, smiling.

'We've got to keep a cool head,' Natalie reminded everyone. 'If we do, and Steggy's on the same form as yesterday, we've got a good chance of winning.'

'Speaking of Steggy,' said Charlie, untying the tent flaps, 'let's go and see how the dinosaurs are. We want them on top form for the final.'

When they reached the dinosaurs, Fing, Mimi and Spud were all awake and eating their breakfast.

'Where's Steggy?' asked Natalie, but none of the dinosaurs seemed to know.

'He must have gone to the dinoloo,' said Charlie. 'I'm sure he'll be back soon.'

But by the time Charlie and his friends had finished their breakfast of cold mammoth meat sausages washed down with a beaker of mammoth milk, there was still no sign of him.

'Perhaps he's gone to the dinoball pitch to get a good viewing spot for the runners-up match,' suggested Natalie. The Fangbury Flyers and Talontree Tornadoes were due to play each other later that morning for third and fourth place. Charlie was sure Steggy would want to watch.

He headed off towards the dinoball pitch to find him, but when he got there, Steggy was nowhere to be seen. As the supporters made their way up to the pitch to get ready for the first match, Charlie kept a watchful eye out for Steggy. When he saw his mum and dad in the crowd he ran over to ask if his dinosaur friend was at home. They shook their heads – they hadn't seen him since the day before.

The nearer it got to tail-swipe, the more Charlie began to suspect that something was wrong. Steggy wouldn't have missed watching the runners-up match without a really good reason. When his team-mates arrived to take up their viewing positions, Charlie told them he was going to search the town.

As the game got underway, Charlie ran down the hill to Sabreton. He looked in every window and in all of Steggy's favourite 'hide and seek' hiding spots but he couldn't find him. By the half-time trumpet, the Fangbury Flyers were one-nil up and Charlie had looked everywhere he could think of. His stomach lurched as he began to realise that something terrible had happened. He ran back to the pitch, hoping that Steggy might have turned up safe and sound to watch the match, but Steggy still wasn't there.

'He's not in the town,' said Charlie to his team-mates. 'I'm going to see if I can find any tracks.'

'You can't!' spluttered James, 'That will take ages! There's only a short lunch break between this match and the final.'

'Without Steggy we don't have a chance of winning the final,' mumbled Leo.

James bit his lip. Leo was right. Steggy had to be found.

'I'll come with you,' said Billy. 'I'm the best hunter in Sabreton – you'll need my skills to help find Steggy's tracks.'

'But you're our reserve player,' said Natalie. 'With Charlie and Steggy gone, you and Fang are on the team.'

'I'm *one* of the reserve players,' corrected Billy. 'Tommy and Gally will have to play instead.' Billy turned to Charlie. 'We need to start where we last saw Steggy.'

'The campsite,' said Charlie.

'Right,' said Billy, calling Fang and heading off in that direction.

'What'll we tell Mrs Heavystep?' shouted Natalie.

Their teacher was getting ready to referee the second

half of the runners-up match and knew nothing about Steggy's disappearance.

'I'm sure you'll think of something,' called Charlie over his shoulder.

The rest of the Sureshots watched the boys leave and James said what they were all thinking.

'They'd better be back by tail-swipe or we haven't got a chance of winning the cup.'

CHAPTER 14

Charlie and Billy were crouching on the ground by the Sureshots' tent looking for clues when Charlie heard a roar come from the dinoball pitch. The second half of the runners-up match was underway and they had no time to lose.

'Dinosaurs don't just disappear,' explained Billy as he examined the dusty ground carefully. 'Clues are always left behind. That's what makes me such a good hunter, A good hunter is a good tracker too.'

Charlie nodded – he was glad to have his friend with him. 'What are we looking for?' he asked.

'Anything out of the ordinary! A-ha!' Billy pointed

to the ground in triumph.

Charlie looked. All he could see was grass and dust. There wasn't anything special about that. Then he looked again. There were dinosaur tracks in the dust. They were faint but they were there, and next to them were some other peculiar tracks.

'These dinosaur prints are stegosaurus tracks,' said Billy, nodding to himself. 'But what are these?' Billy pointed at the strange tracks. They were long and smooth and didn't have any claws marks. 'They don't belong to any dinosaur I know.'

Charlie's blood ran cold. If Billy didn't recognise the prints then what strange creature did they belong to? Had they taken Steggy? Perhaps his friend was in trouble. It was up to Charlie to find him.

'Come on, Billy!' said Charlie, scurrying off in the direction of the prints. 'There's no time to lose.'

'Wait!' shouted Billy. 'We can ride Fang. He's strong enough to carry both of us and it'll be much quicker.'

Billy clambered up on to the dinosaur's back and then reached out a hand to help Charlie. When he got up on Fang's back, Charlie put his arms around his strong friend's waist and held on tight as Fang set off to follow the prints.

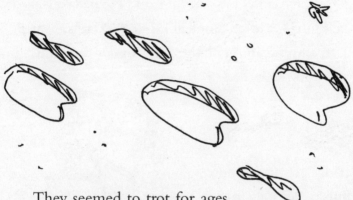

They seemed to trot for ages. They followed the prints out past Charlie's dinoloos and into the wilderness that lay between Sabreton and T. Rex Mountain. Charlie's mind began to race as they went. The sun was halfway across the sky – the first match would be almost over and the cup final would begin soon. He felt bad for leaving his friends but he hoped they understood. Steggy was more important than any dinoball cup.

Back at the dinoball pitch, the first match was over.

Fangbury had won two-nil and the large crowd was eagerly looking forward to the final. Some of them had painted their faces, some of them were blowing on shell horns and most were wearing the team colours of either Sabreton or Tuskville on their furskins or painted on their faces.

'I look ridiculous,' said Tommy as he stood beside his team-mates, gazing down at his tunic. He had squeezed himself into Charlie's dinoball kit. It was far too small for him and his tummy bulged out under the skins.

'You look fine,' lied Leo.

Tommy stared at him angrily.

'It doesn't matter how he looks,' said Natalie quickly. 'All that matters is that he plays the match.'

Tommy sighed and patted Gally on the neck. 'For Sabreton,' he said.

There was a noisy ripping sound as Tommy threw his leg over the dinosaur's back.

'That's torn it,' sniggered Cuthbert Polish as he and the Tuskville team trotted past in their pristine yellow and white kits, pointing to the large rip in Tommy's kit.

Tommy began to blush.
'Just ignore him,' Natalie hissed. 'We'll soon show him who's boss when we get on that pitch.'

As the Sureshots made their way towards the centre circle, a cheer went up from the home supporters. It was followed by one or two nervous murmurs when the crowd noticed Charlie and Steggy weren't with them. Mrs Heavystep ran over to see what was going on and Natalie did her best to explain. They all hoped Charlie and Billy would manage to find Steggy and get back soon. Tommy and Gally would do their best, but everyone remembered that Gally had missed the goal in the Sureshot trials – they were no comparison to Steggy and Charlie. If the Sureshots were to have any chance at all they needed their star striker.

Under the shadow of T. Rex Mountain, Fang had stopped and the two boys were scouring the ground for more clues. The ground was less dusty out by the mountain and they had lost the tracks they had been following.

'There's nothing here!' said Charlie with a rueful shake of the head.

Billy tutted and looked at Charlie. 'And I thought you were supposed to be clever,' he sighed. 'We may have lost these tracks, but there are other signs if you know where to look.' Billy nodded towards a grove filled with bushes. 'They went through there.'

'How do you know?'

'Look again.'

Charlie looked again where Billy pointed. He could see that some of the branches and brambles had been bent back. 'Someone's made a path,' he gasped, pointing.

Billy nodded and smiled. 'We'll make a hunter out of you yet, Charlie Flint! Come on!'

Billy jumped back on to Fang and pulled Charlie up behind him. The dinosaur made his way carefully through the brambles and prickles. As they passed a

particularly prickly bush, Charlie spotted something. 'Look at this!' he hissed, tearing a piece of furskin from the bushes. 'Whoever is with Steggy must have snagged themselves.'

Charlie held the cloth up to the light.

'That's strange,' said Billy looking at the furskin. 'It's been dyed white and yellow. It looks a little bit like a Tuskville dinoball kit.'

Charlie's heart skipped a beat. 'I think it *is* a Tuskville dinoball kit,' he gulped. Then Charlie slapped his forehead. 'Of course!'

'What?' asked Billy.

'I know what, or should I say *who*, made those tracks we found next to Steggy's at the campsite.'

Billy looked confused.

'When he first arrived, Cuthbert Polish showed us his shoes,' explained Charlie.

'What are shoes?' asked Billy.

'They're all the rage in Tuskville,' said Charlie sarcastically. 'They're leather things to protect the soles of your feet. But he's the only person in Sabreton to have a pair, so he must have something to do with Steggy's disappearance.'

'Why would he want Steggy to disappear?'

'When he was refereeing our dinoball match yesterday he would have been in a perfect position to see how good Steggy was at scoring goals. With Steggy out of the way, the Tuskville Terrors should have no problem winning the dinoball cup!'

Billy gasped. It all made sense. He urged Fang to move a little quicker. Once they got out of the bramble bushes the trail disappeared again. Charlie and Billy looked for more clues as to where they might have gone.

'Gotcha!' said Charlie suddenly.

He bent down and picked up a little stone holding it up for Billy to see.

Billy scratched his head.

'It's a cherry stone!' explained Charlie, smiling. 'But there aren't any cherry trees around here, so where did it come from?'

Billy shrugged his shoulders. 'Search me!'

'It came from Cuthbert Polish,' said Charlie triumphantly. 'He loves them.'

'He loves them quite a lot,' said Billy pointing to a scattered trail of cherry stones that led across a large grassy plain. 'If we follow that trail, we'll find Steggy.'

As Fang carried them across the grassy plain, Billy turned to Charlie. 'I think I know where we're heading,' he said quietly.

'Where?' asked Charlie.

'On the other side of this plain is the Bog of Ooze,' said Billy with a grim shake of his head.

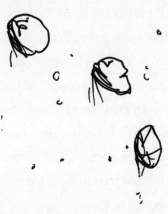

Charlie's heart froze. Cuthbert knew all about the Bog of Ooze and how dangerous it was. It was just the sort of place an unlucky dinosaur could get stranded. If Steggy had been left in the Bog of Ooze then they may already be too late.

'Can't Fang go any faster?' said Charlie, patting the big dinosaur on the neck. 'We've no time to waste!'

Back at the dinoball pitch, the cup final had got off to a crunching start. At first, the Sureshots had defended as if their lives depended on it. But soon the Terrors had started to use their dirty tricks against them.

They targeted Leo, the smallest player, first. Spud was running with the ball when Spitball barged straight into them. In the kerfuffle, Spud received a nasty scratch on his neck. Leo protested to the referees but both agreed it had probably been an accident. Leo and the rest of the Sureshots knew better.

Tommy and Gally were doing their best as replacement strikers, but they lacked Steggy and Charlie's speed and skill. The team desperately needed Steggy and Charlie back.

Mimi soon had her foot stamped on and James was pushed off

Fing altogether. He crouched on the ground and covered his head with his arms as the Tuskville Terrors thundered all around him.

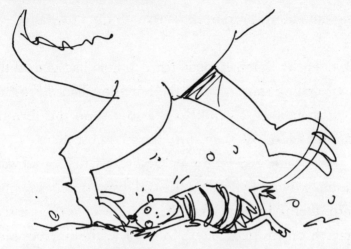

'This is terrible!' he moaned when he was safely seated on his dinosaur's back once again.

'We're doomed,' agreed Leo.

Just then one of the Terrors zoomed past on the wing to score the first goal of the match and the home crowd fell silent. The Sabreton Sureshots hung their heads in despair. As Natalie rolled the ball towards the centre circle she looked at her team. They were battered, bruised and bewildered and didn't have their star striker. They looked as if they had already been beaten. If Charlie didn't get back soon, the Sureshots didn't stand a chance.

CHAPTER 15

'There he is!' shouted Charlie as he leapt off Fang and ran towards the Bog of Ooze.

Steggy looked up. His four legs were stuck fast in the thick black mud of the bog. As Charlie watched him struggle, he seemed to sink a little further.

'Not so fast!' shouted Billy, grabbing Charlie by the shoulder and yanking him to a halt. 'This place is dangerous. Some bits sink faster than others. You have to be careful.'

Billy tossed one of the cherry stones into the bog. It disappeared beneath the thick black mud with a squelch.

Charlie shuddered – that could have been him.

There were lots of rumours surrounding the Bog of Ooze. Some said it was bottomless and you'd keep on sinking forever if you wandered on to it, others said that you'd get stuck fast and starve to death.

'We need to get him out before he sinks to the bottom!' cried Charlie.

'And so we can get him back to play in the Dinoball Cup,' reminded Billy.

Charlie had forgotten all about the cup. Rescuing his friend was the only thing that mattered to him.

'Any ideas?'

Billy grinned. 'We'll have him out in no time.'

The muscly caveboy reached up for Fang's vine reins, and began to untie them.

'When I rescued Fing and Fang from the bog I used a vine lasso. I had to pull pretty hard though. Hopefully with Fang and you to help, things will be a little bit easier.'

Billy tied a loop in the vine and began to swing it over his head while Steggy looked on nervously.

Carefully, Billy tiptoed

to the edge of the bog and let the rope fly. Charlie held his breath as he watched it sail through the air. The rope bounced off Steggy's back and landed in the mud with a splat.

Charlie shook his head in despair.

'Nearly,' said Billy, pulling the rope back towards him. 'Try and stick your tail up, Steggy,' he called. 'It'll give me something to aim for!'

Steggy did what as he was told and stuck his tail high in the air.

Billy swished the rope over his head again. He flung it towards the trapped dinosaur. Steggy moved his tail from side to side trying to anticipate where the rope was going to land. This time Billy's aim was better and the lasso slipped over Steggy's tail.

'Well done, Billy!' shouted Charlie.

'He's not out of the swamp yet,' warned Billy. 'Now the hard work starts. We need to pull.'

Billy tied the other end of the rope around one of Fang's front feet and together the two caveboys and the dinosaur began to heave on the vine with all their might.

The rope creaked as they pulled. Sweat poured down Charlie's forehead and Billy clenched his teeth with the effort until there was a loud *plop*, and one of Steggy's feet came free.

'That's it!' groaned Billy. 'Keep on pulling!'

They yanked and tugged until they heard another *plop*, then another as Steggy's feet popped out of the mud. Soon all four of Steggy's feet were out of the mud and he was pulled across the bog on his bottom.

When his feet touched solid ground he ran over and covered Charlie in happy licks.

'I missed you too!' said Charlie as he tried to catch his breath. 'We've made a mess of your dinopants!'

Steggy turned to try and see. His dinopants were covered in thick brown mud.

'We haven't got time to worry about that now!' said

Billy leaping on to Fang's back. 'You two have a dinoball cup to win!'

Steggy yelped in excitement and crouched down to let Charlie clamber on to his back. As he and Steggy followed Billy and Fang back to Sabreton, Charlie could only hope he'd be in time to teach Cuthbert Polish and the Tuskville Terrors the lesson they deserved.

CHAPTER 16

'That was terrible!' moaned Leo as he slid off Spud's back.

'And embarrassing,' agreed Natalie.

It was half-time in the Dinoball Cup Final and the Sabreton Sureshots were two goals down. They were sitting on the ground behind the goalposts nursing all sorts of cuts and bruises. Some of the home crowd were so sure their team were going to lose they had even started to head back down to Sabreton.

'Sorry, guys,' said Tommy. 'Me and Gally just aren't good enough. Mrs Heavystep was right – Charlie and Steggy are the better players.'

'I wish they were here now,' said James sadly.

'Did someone say my name?' called a voice behind them.

The Sureshots turned to see Charlie, Steggy, Billy and Fang standing by the goalposts. They couldn't believe their eyes.

'Can I have my kit back, Tommy? I think it fits me better!'

Tommy tugged off the purple and pink kit. 'Never liked it anyway,' he said.

'You found Steggy!' Natalie smiled as she gave him a stroke. 'Where was he?'

'I'll explain all that later,' said Charlie, pulling on his tunic. 'After we've thrashed those Tuskville Terrors.'

With a cheer the Sureshots made their way back on to the pitch.

Cuthbert Polish was shocked to see Steggy taking up his position for the second half.

'You!' he spluttered. 'How?'

But Charlie was in no mood for explanations. The referees tooted their trumpets and the second half began. Charlie and Steggy had a point to prove and they got stuck into the game immediately. Steggy may have had a traumatic morning but he managed to put it all behind him. He skilfully used his tail to manoeuvre the ball on to his foot and hurtled towards the goal. The air around Sabreton rang to the sound of thundering dinosaurs.

'Over here!' called Leo as he and Spud made a crafty run up the wing.

Steggy hoofed the ball over the heads of the Tuskville defenders and Spud headed the ball towards goal. In an instant Steggy saw what Spud was up to and made a run to connect with the ball. Charlie steered Steggy round the Tuskville defence, holding on for dear life as Steggy leapt into the air and knocked the ball into the goal. The crowd cheered in delight.

'That's one,' said Charlie triumphantly. 'Now for the others.'

Suddenly Steggy was all over the pitch as he twisted and turned, trying to find a clear route through to the Tuskville goal. When Fing kicked the ball into an open space, Steggy saw his chance and bolted.

Craig Shredder saw what Steggy was up to and gritted his teeth. He wasn't going to let him get there. He and Spitball charged, Spitball let out a deafening scream and bared his teeth. Charlie saw the fearsome dinosaur heading towards them and tried to move out of the way – but it was too late. Spitball collided with Steggy in a crunching tackle. Charlie was thrown from his dinosaur and landed in a heap on the ground. The crowd gasped. That had been nasty. Clive Spittle tooted his trumpet for a free kick.

'What?' spluttered Craig, leaping from Spitball to argue with the referee. 'You must be blind as well as hairy! You farmers always were a bit thick!'

Clive turned red with anger. Nobody spoke to him like that! He tooted once again and pointed to the sideline. He was sending Craig off the pitch.

'No way!' growled Craig. 'I'm not going.'

Clive wasn't listening. If the caveboy wouldn't leave on his own he'd just have to give him a hand. Clive whistled to his diplodocus, who reached his long neck into the pitch, grabbed Craig by the scruff of his furskin, and dangled him high in the air as he continued to watch the game.

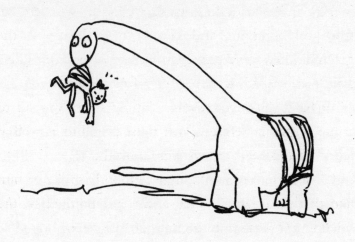

'Let's see how they do with three men!' Natalie said, laughing.

Without their captain, the Terrors lost all of their form. Steggy dodged through their defence like it wasn't there and powered the ball into the goal before the goalie had a chance to move. The crowd roared with delight. Two-two.

Craig tried to shout instructions but his team were too rattled to listen. Jim Hawk looked up at the sun. There were only a few moments of the game remaining. He put his trumpet to his lips, waiting for the sun to reach the fifth tree on the horizon.

Billy saw what was happening. 'Charlie!' he shouted. 'Look!'

Charlie saw the trumpet in Jim's mouth and realised they had moments to go. 'Everybody forward!' he shouted. 'We can win this!'

Leo, James and Natalie left their defensive positions and charged for the goal. The Tuskville Terrors didn't know what hit them. As Spud kicked the ball into the centre of the pitch, Fing ran circles around the defence while Mimi darted up the middle. Natalie whooped as her dinosaur sped towards the ball. Steggy had found space up by the goal line and was just waiting for the pass. Charlie saw Jim's chest bulge as he drew breath. He was going to toot any moment! Mimi connected with the ball. Charlie watched it fly towards him and urged Steggy upwards. Steggy leapt and lunged for the ball with a spectacular overhead kick. Charlie clung on as he spun in mid-air. Steggy's foot connected with the ball and it sailed into the goal, just as Jim blew for full-time.

Steggy landed back on his feet and bowed while the crowd cheered and blew their honking shells. Mrs Heavystep and Boris danced a little jig together. The Sabreton Sureshots had done it. They'd won the Dinoball Cup!

CHAPTER 17

After the mayor had presented the team with the trophy, Charlie explained what had happened to Steggy. He produced the white and yellow cloth to prove he was telling the truth and Boris frog-marched Cuthbert up to the campsite to check his shoes against the prints Billy and Charlie had seen in the dust. They matched perfectly.

Cuthbert looked at the ground. 'I was only doing it for the good of Tuskville!' he spluttered. 'How does it look to be beaten by a load of bumpkins?'

The rest of the Tuskville Terrors had known nothing about it and immediately sacked him as their coach.

Leslie Trumpbottom also promised to tell the mayor of Tuskville what had happened next time he saw him. Cuthbert turned pale.

Once the presentation was over, the mayor declared that the rest of the day was going to be given over to a feast to celebrate the Sureshots' wonderful victory. Charlie and the Sureshots discussed the highs and lows of the competition with the Fangbury Flyers and the Talontree Tornadoes – and this time the Tuskville Terrors joined in too. They weren't a bad bunch after all – even Craig Shredder was all right once you got to know him. Well, pretty much.

As Charlie walked past the Town Hall back to his cave later, the mayor popped his head through the window.

'All set for next year?' he called.

'Next year?' asked Charlie. 'Can we do it again?'

'Of course!' said the mayor with a smile. 'I think the Dinoball Cup was one of my best ideas ever!'

Charlie rolled his eyes. He wasn't about to argue. If the mayor wanted to think that the cup was his idea then that was fine.

When Charlie lay in his bed later that night, he was already dreaming about scoring the winning goal in next year's Dinoball Cup.

Don't miss the rest of Charlie Flint's inventions and adventures...

DINOPANTS

Caveboy Charlie Flint is fed up with dinosaurs leaving poo all over his home town of Sabreton. When he finds his brand new club covered in dinopoo, it's the final straw. Something must be done – so Charlie invents Dinopants!

But will he manage to convince the dinosaurs to put on a pair of his fantastic new Dinopants? And what about the terrifying T-Rex who is determined to make both the pants and Charlie extinct?

'Fast moving fun adventure admirably complemented by Richard Morgan's hilarious drawings.'
School Librarian